# OH SNOW

by Monica Mayper
pictures by June Otani

HarperCollins*Publishers*

The paintings were done with a pen line and an oil wash.

Oh Snow
Text copyright © 1991 by Monica Mayper
Illustrations copyright © 1991 by June Otani
Printed in the U.S.A. All rights reserved.
1  2  3  4  5  6  7  8  9  10
First Edition

Library of Congress Cataloging-in-Publication Data
Mayper, Monica.
  Oh snow / by Monica Mayper ; pictures by June Otani.
    p.     cm.
  Summary: A young child enjoys a new snowfall outside.
  ISBN 0-06-024203-5. — ISBN 0-06-024204-3 (lib. bdg.)
  [1. Snow—Fiction.]  I. Otani, June, ill.   II. Title.
PZ7.M47373Oh   1991                              90-42088
[E]—dc20                                              CIP
                                                      AC

To my Minnesota goddaughter,
Darcy Elizabeth Ward—

may she love snow!

—M. M.

For Ansel

—J. O.

Out my window,
snow.

Light of snow
gray-bright of snow

hush of snow

wind-rush of snow—

I watch its slow
falling
falling
falling
falling.

The whole world is white sky
come down for me to be in.

I am a tree.
My boots are roots.
My arms are branches catching sky.

My cold skin sings
to the touch of feathery things.

In my tree heart starts
a new green shout
that must come out
that WILL come out!

OH SNOW   oh snow   oh snow

I'm ant-small at the edge of a silent field.
I stamp giant's tracks where no one's been.

I lie on my back—
My arms are wings.

I flap and float—

under me, buried deep,
Spring's asleep!
Spring's asleep!

See a chickadee at the feeder
peck seed turn peck peck seed.

See my steam-wisp of whistle—
here comes the next-door dog
bound wallow bound wallow shake shake.

See us fall
roll over roll over down hill
bark
laugh—

Hear my spring-green shout—
You must come out!
Come out! Come out!

63

JP
MAYPER, MONICA
OH SNOW

(04) (07) (03)

(05) (07)   11

12   13

14

17   15

4/92